A Mouse's Tail

Published by Stairwell Books on behalf of
The Red Tower CIC
Foss Islands Road
York
YO31 7UL

redtoweryork.org.uk
@RedTowerYork1

ISBN: 978-1-913432-69-0

p0

Red Tower: A Mouse's Tail

By Millie Oram (artwork), Chloe Bennison (book design)
and Ellie Mullaney (text)

Acknowledgements

We would like to thank York St John University for providing the means
to produce this book. Millie, Chloe and Ellie are students at the University
and have been enabled to write the book via work experience and an
internship. Millie studies animation; Chloe, English Language and Linguistics;
and Ellie, History.

Thanks also to David Scott, a primary specialist at York St John University,
for providing feedback on the manuscript.

The project has been managed by the Red Tower Community Interest
Company with a view to providing younger residents and visitors some
idea of the historical background to a well-loved feature of the City
Walls.

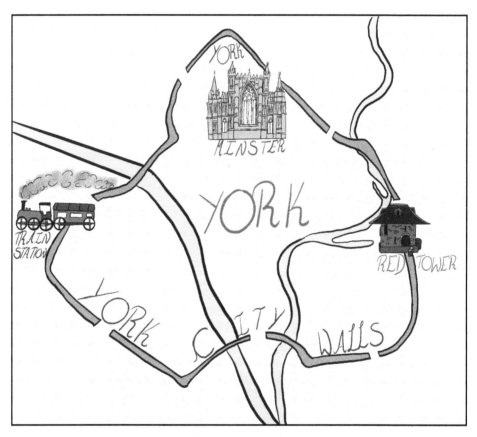

Map of York

Chapter 1

Brieanna scampered across the grass to the Red Tower.
She was excited. She loved visiting her Grandpa and Grandma so much.

Her grandparents were at the door to meet her.

"Hello, Brieanna." said Grandpa.

"Hello, Grandpa, Grandma."

"Come, in, come in", said Grandma.

Brieanna went through the little door and into the Red Tower.

She loved it. It was on the city walls and was over five hundred years old. The mice family had lived there since it was built in 1490. They lived under the Tower where the humans did not go. The family had come over from France with William the Conqueror in 1066.

They went into the dining room for tea. Grandma had prepared a huge pile of cheese sandwiches.

After tea, Grandpa got up.

"Brieanna, come and see my new invention".

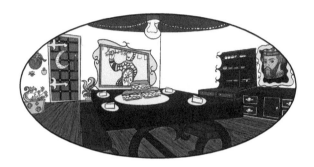

Grandpa was an inventor and Brieanna loved his crazy ideas. "What is it, Grandpa?"

"It's a time machine."

"Wow!" said the little mouse. "Can I see it?"

"Of course, little one. Follow me."

They went to the workshop.
In front of them was a huge machine with a big red button.
Beside it, a sign with big letters:

DO NOT TOUCH!

Grandpa explained that it did work but was not ready.

He looked at Brieanna and said,

"You won't touch it, will you?"

"No, Grandpa."

Grandma said it was time for bed.
They read some stories and then Brieanna brushed her
teeth, put on her pyjamas, and went off to her bed.

She couldn't sleep.
She was excited by the invention.
She kept thinking about the time machine.

If only she could travel in time. What would she see? Who
would she meet?

When all the house was quiet, Brieanna got up, got dressed
and went to the workshop.

She switched on the light.

There was the time machine. There was the big red button.
There was the sign with big letters:

DO NOT TOUCH!

She stared at the time machine and rubbed her whiskers.

Her paw was moving closer to the big red button.

She closed her eyes and her paw pressed
the button.

Brieanna was gone …

Chapter 2

Brieanna was lying on the grass. At first, she could only see a bright white light.

Then she saw the city walls. But, where was the Red Tower?

Everywhere there was noise and shouting. The workmen were dressed in funny clothes. There were no proper roads, no shops, no cars. Carts were transporting bricks and people were digging.

Where was she? What had happened?

Brieanna was frightened. She wanted to be in her warm bed. She wanted to see Grandpa and Grandma again.

She hid and tried to decide what to do.

In the morning, Grandma took a drink to Brieanna's bedroom as usual. She opened the door. The bed was empty.

Where was Brieanna?

"Bert", she cried. "Bert, come here quickly". (Grandpa's real name was Camembert, but everybody called him Bert.)

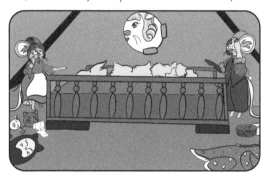

Grandpa came scurrying along the corridor.

"Brieanna's gone!" "Where can she be?"

Grandpa thought of a moment. "She can't have gone to the workshop, can she?"

They rushed to the workshop. The light was on and the big red button was flashing!

"Oh, no!" cried Grandma. "Look what you have done!" Grandpa rubbed his whiskers, shook his head.

"Bert, you'll have to fix it." Bert just stared at the machine.

At the same time, Brieanna was looking for the Red Tower. She saw a mouse not far away. The mouse was dressed in strange clothes. Brieanna went up to her.

"Hello, mouse. Can you tell me where the Red Tower is?"

"Hello. This is a new tower that they are building with bricks. Is this what you are looking for? The bricks are red."

Brieanna had an idea. Could Grandpa's machine have worked?

Could she have travelled back in time?

If this is the Red Tower being built, it must be 1490. They are building the Red Tower next to the walls.

Brieanna thanked the mouse and said goodbye. She looked around her.

Brieanna was scared. She wanted her Grandpa.

Grandma and Grandpa will be so worried.

Brieanna turned around. Some men were coming towards her with shovels. They were coming nearer and nearer.

Brieanna went towards a crack in the walls.

Everything went black. Brieanna was gone ...

Chapter 3

Brieanna opened her eyes.

There was smoke in the air. She could hear the cannons firing. Bullets were flying past her.

Inside the city walls there were men with floppy hats.

In the distance, there were men wearing hard round helmets.

They were firing cannons towards the walls.

A voice shouted,

"Come over here little girl!"

A mouse with a floppy hat was shouting from near the Red Tower.

Brieanna ran towards the mouse and they dived into a hole in the wall.

"Phew, that was close." said the mouse.
Brieanna soon calmed down.

"What is happening?" asked Brieanna. "What year is this?"

"It's 1644, of course", he chuckled. "We're defending the city for the king".

Brieanna knew about the civil war from school and understood.

"Where are you from, little girl?"

"I come from near here but from another time. My Grandpa and Grandma live in the Red Tower but many years later."
The mouse looked puzzled.

At that moment, Brieanna remembered her Grandpa and Grandma. "They must be very worried", she said.

She thought about a big plate of cheese sandwiches and her warm bed.

Outside, they could hear the fighting getting nearer. The cannonballs were whistling by. The walls were shaking and the stones were falling all around.

"Look out!" shouted the mouse. A big stone was falling on Brieanna's head.

She fainted.

Everything went black...

Chapter 4

Brieanna opened her eyes.

There were no more cannons and no more guns.
The Red Tower was almost in ruins. There was no roof.
She could see some builders with a pile of old bricks.
They were long and thin. There were some plans of a building.

Brieanna recognised the Red Tower. She could see the
sloping roof, the windows and a new door.

Brieanna went into the old building.

She saw that one wall was missing. It was dirty and smelly.

A voice called out.

"Hey little mouse! What are you doing here?"

Brieanna turned round and there was an old mouse standing there. He looked like Grandpa.

"I'm lost" said Brieanna.

"Come here, little girl. Come and meet my wife and family."

Brieanna followed the family down to the cellar under the Red Tower.

This part of the Red Tower had not been touched by the builders. The old mouse introduced the family.

He explained that the family had lived there since it was built. He said that the family had come over with William the Conqueror. Brieanna smiled. She knew the story.

"What are they doing?" asked Brieanna.

"Well" explained the old man, "The Red Tower has been used as a store. It has also been used to keep animals. The builders are going to make it nice. The old bricks are long and thin. They are going to put them on the outside".

They went outside again. Brieanna could see now how the Red Tower got to look as it did.

Brieanna could hear a noise. The noise got louder and louder and Brieanna could hear workmen digging.

"We have to get out." shouted the old man.

The walls were crumbling. The ground was shaking. There was dust everywhere.

Brieanna ran out and across the ground. A workman was chasing her with a stick.

Everything went black...

Chapter 5

Brieanna suddenly felt wet all over.

She was floating in the water.

She panicked. She couldn't swim.

She could see the top of the Red Tower. The water came halfway up the walls.

She heard a boat behind her.

She waved her arms and shouted in her little mouse voice.

A human scooped Brieanna out of the water. She was put in the
red rubber boat. It had a big red motor behind it.

She wasn't alone in the boat. There was an old lady, a dog and a
parrot in a cage. Everything looked modern. The houses looked
modern. The people were wearing modern clothes.

The boat took Brieanna to safety near the Red Tower.

Brieanna thanked the man.
She looked around and everywhere was flooded.
Cars were under water. The streets were under water.

Brieanna shouted to a family of hedgehogs that she recognised. They were neighbours of the Red Tower and knew her Grandparents.

"What's happening?"

"The Rover Foss has flooded and people have had to leave their houses" replied the hedgehog.

Brieanna remembered her grandparents talking about the floods in 2015. They had been away from the Red Tower on that day. She knew they were safe.

"Do you want to come with us?

"Yes, please". Brieanna hopped on the raft.

The hedgehog family took her for a ride around the walls.

"Where do you live, little girl?

"I live near here but I was staying with my grandparents. You know Bert, don't you?"

"Of course we do. Lovely to meet you."

Brieanna looked at the Red Tower under water. She knew it was not safe. She did not know where to go.

She stayed with the hedgehog family rescuing other animals. She was tired and wet and wanted to be back home.

Suddenly, Brieanna heard a noise.

It was the boat returning with some more people. The boat passed by the little raft. Brieanna fell overboard.

Everything went black …

Chapter 6

Brieanna opened her eyes slowly.

Where was she now? What time was she in?

She looked across the room and could see the red button and the time machine. She looked around and there was Grandpa looking very worried.

"Grandpa, Grandpa", said Brieanna.

Grandpa turned round in surprise.

"Brieanna, my little one. Where have you been?"

"I've been back in time. I saw them building the Red Tower, I was there during the Civil War …"

"Slow down, Brieanna".

"Really Grandpa, I was there when they built the sloping roof and put the old bricks on the outside of the building. I saw the floods and was nearly drowned."

"What an adventure! Come and tell us all about it."

Brieanna went to the dining room with Grandpa to see Grandma.

Grandma had been crying all day and was holding her wet hanky in her paw.

Grandma jumped for joy when she saw her and hugged her tight.

Grandpa said "Let's see what we can find to eat. The humans are having a barbeque today. There is bound to be lots of food".

They went outside. It was beginning to get dark.

There were lots of people in front of the Red Tower. There was music and lots of people talking.

"Come on. There must be some cheese for our supper".

Brieanna, Grandpa and Grandma sat on the grass and helped themselves to the food.

Grandpa looked at Brieanna and said "Now then. Tell us about your adventures".

Brieanna told the whole story of her time travel. Grandpa and Grandma looked on in amazement.

"Do you promise not to touch the red button ever again", said Grandma.

"I promise."

Brieanna paused and said "Do you have to tell my mum about my adventures?"

"Would she believe you?" replied Grandma.

"Probably not" said Brieanna with a grin.

The three mice hugged each other.

Ingram Content Group UK Ltd.
Milton Keynes UK
UKHW052147030423
419585UK00010B/82

9 781913 432690